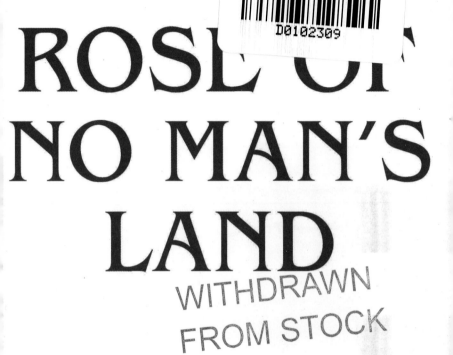

ROSE OF NO MAN'S LAND

ANNE PERRY

A Timepiece Novel

To Scuff

First published in 2011 in Great Britain by
Barrington Stoke Ltd
18 Walker Street, Edinburgh, EH3 7LP

www.barringtonstoke.co.uk

ISBN: 978-1-84299-487-0

Printed in China by Leo

Contents

Chapter 1
Back Again

Mr Jones' voice droned on and on about the politics and events that had led to World War One. Maybe some people in the class could follow what he was saying, but Rosie was almost in tears trying to make sense of it. It was complicated, so Mr Jones had put all the names and places and stuff on the whiteboard to help. Of course, that didn't help Rosie at all, as she couldn't read any of it.

Something amazing had happened to Rosie when the class had studied the Tudors. It must have been a dream, but at the time she was convinced that she had gone back in time to the Spanish Armada and met Queen Elizabeth the First. That seemed a million years ago now. Here she was, back in history class, lost and stupid because she couldn't read.

Gary Hodder had started to twist around at his desk and flick bits of old chewing gum at one of the girls. One bit missed and sailed past Rosie to land on Mr Jones' shoes. Mr Jones turned round and glared at Rosie.

"Rosie Sands!" he said. "You will stay after class to pick that up. And you can clean the desks while you're at it to show you're sorry."

"But, sir, it wasn't me!" Rosie protested.

"Of course it wasn't," Mr Jones replied, in a voice that made it clear he thought it was. "It never is you, Rosie. As I said, you can stay behind."

Stacey Summers pulled some new gum out of her pocket and gave it to Rosie. "Go on," she said. "If you have to stay anyway, you might as well really hit him."

Everyone laughed.

"That's enough from you, too, Stacey," Mr Jones said crossly. "Any more lip and you'll be staying as well." He turned back to the board.

The rest of the class was awful for Rosie. She wanted to cry but instead she had to sit and listen to even more facts about the silly arguments that had led to the war. Then, when the bell went, the others left and she had to stay behind.

Stacey waved at Rosie on the way out the door. "See ya, babe," she said.

Zack Edwards was the last to leave. He stopped at the door and turned to look at Rosie.

"That was a bit rough, Rosie," he said. "It was obvious it wasn't you."

Rosie went red. "Thanks," she said. "It doesn't matter, really."

"Maybe catch you later," said Zack.

Rosie didn't know what to say. Zack was the hottest boy in school – and he had stopped to talk to her! He was really clever, too, and he normally only went out with the clever girls. Well, there was no danger he'd want to go out with Rosie. She couldn't even read, and she turned into a red-faced, stammering loser any time he spoke to her.

As Zack left, Mr Jones came back in.

"So what are we going to do with you, Rosie?" he asked. He didn't look cross any more.

"I'll clean the desks," Rosie said. "But it really wasn't me."

"I know," Mr Jones said.

"What?" Rosie asked, confused.

"I know you didn't throw the gum," said Mr Jones. "I'm sorry I pretended that I thought you did. But I wanted a word with you and I didn't want to do it in front of everyone else."

Rosie frowned. "What about?" she asked.

"I've noticed that you try to get away without answering questions in class," Mr Jones said. "And I know you're a clever girl – just think about that talk you did about Queen Elizabeth. So I started to wonder if there's another problem that's stopping you from taking part."

Rosie went red again. "What do you mean? There's no problem."

"Do you know that lots of people find it hard to read?" asked Mr Jones. "Some were just off school and missed something and then have never had a chance to catch up. A lot have dyslexia, which can make it hard to remember what words look like. Whatever the reason, there are lots of ways to help."

Rosie felt tears sting her eyes. Her whole body was hot with shame. "What's that got to do with me?" she asked. "I'm not some retard."

"That's not a nice word, Rosie," said Mr Jones, but he didn't sound angry. "And just because you have a problem with reading, it doesn't mean you're stupid."

"I can read fine, thanks," said Rosie.

Mr Jones looked at her for another minute, then he smiled. "Well. I think you can go now. But remember, I'm always here if you change your mind."

Rosie grabbed her bag and ran out of the room as fast as she could. Before she had made it to the door there were hot tears streaming down her cheeks.

Chapter 2
The Upside-down Watch

That Saturday Rosie went into town alone. She had something to return.

She walked up the High Street and stopped outside a little antique shop with a window full of watches and clocks. The door was locked but Rosie peered through the glass to see if there was anybody in. There was a faint glow right at the back of the shop, so she knocked on the glass.

A few seconds later the door opened a crack and a man with bright blue eyes peeked out.

"It's Rosie, isn't it?" the man asked. He smiled. "Come in, come in."

Rosie let him usher her into the shop and then waited as he went to turn on the lights.

"Now, Rosie, how can I help you?" the man asked.

"I think I must have taken this by mistake," Rosie said. She held out her hand and showed him the Tudor watch she had found in her bag after the last time she had come to the shop. The very same watch that Queen Elizabeth had given to Rosie in a strange dream, so real that she had been convinced for a while it had actually happened.

"I'm sorry," Rosie said. "I didn't mean to take it. I came lots of times before to give it back, but there was no one here."

The man smiled as he took the watch and held it up to the light.

"What an honest girl you are," he said. "Many people would keep something so valuable. It's beautiful, isn't it?"

Rosie nodded. "Who owned it?" she asked.

"Who knows?" the man said with a smile. "I just look after it. Do you like it?"

"I love it," said Rosie. It was true – it was very hard to give back something so special. The old man was looking at her and smiling, and she thought he knew how she felt.

"I think you deserve a present for your honesty," he said. "Choose one."

He lifted a velvet cloth and Rosie saw three watches lying on a tray. Two were made of gold, very beautiful and ornate. The third one was made of a dark-coloured metal, maybe silver. It didn't have a long chain like the others, just a pin for fixing it on to your clothes.

Straight away Rosie knew that she wanted the third watch. The man smiled when she said so.

"A good choice," he said.

Rosie took the watch from him and held it in her hand. It was warm, like the Tudor watch had been, even though it hadn't been in the window in the sun like the others. She held it up by the pin then looked at the man, confused.

"It's upside down!" she said.

"That's right," said the man. "It's a nurse's watch. It's meant to be pinned to your front, and then you can look at it from above. It's from the Great War."

"When was that?" Rosie asked.

"You perhaps call it World War One," the man said. "1914 to 1918." He looked at his own watch, a normal one on his arm. "Well, Rosie," he said, "I'd love to talk some more, but I have to go. I'm going to look for more watches at a sale this afternoon. I hope you enjoy yours. Take care of it. It's one of my favourites."

"I will," said Rosie. "Thank you so much."

Chapter 3
The Canal

When Rosie got home the rest of the family were out. She went to her room and put the watch on the table beside the bed. Then she took out her history book. She tried and tried to make sense of it, but the more she looked, the more jumbled the words became. The long ones were the worst. She could read them one by one, but it was hard to put them into a sentence that meant anything. It made her head hurt.

She heard the back door slam and her mother call out. Her grandmother was with her too, so Rosie went down to say hello. Her mother had a bag full of shopping. There was a bottle of wine and a big blackcurrant cheesecake. Rosie knew right away that she was planning to make a special dinner.

Rosie chatted to her grandmother while her mother cooked. The food looked great and it was nice to be all together as a family. Then her father phoned to say he'd be late home.

"What?" her mother shouted. "You promised! You know your mum's here today, and you hardly ever see her."

"Oh, don't worry," said Rosie's grandmother. "He's always so busy."

"No," shouted Rosie's mother. "Stop making excuses for him. That's part of the problem – you spoil him."

As soon as she heard that, Rosie knew that her mother and her grandmother were going to fall out, too. She stood up and grabbed her coat.

"I'm not hungry," she said. "I'm off out. Enjoy your cheesecake, Grandma."

"Oh, perfect," her mother said. "You're leaving too. Brilliant."

Rosie felt a bit bad, but not bad enough to stay. Her mum and her grandmother actually got on fine. They would argue about her dad for a bit and then start moaning about other stuff. They enjoyed it but it did Rosie's head in.

At the corner of the next street Rosie met Stacey, who looked bored too. They wandered along the footpath together, not going anywhere special, just away from their homes. In the end, they bought some chips and then found a place to sit and feed the left-overs to the ducks in the canal.

"If I had enough money I'd like to go somewhere, one day," Stacey said. She got out a lip-gloss and started putting it on, then she took a bottle of blue alcopop from her bag and took a swig. She passed the bottle to Rosie.

"Where would you go?" Rosie asked. Not that she really cared, but it was something to talk about. She took a swig of the horrible blue drink.

"I don't know," Stacey said. "Somewhere really different."

"Different from what?" Rosie asked. "Egypt? India? Where?"

"Somewhere with hot men," Stacey said. She looked sideways at Rosie and took the bottle back. "Somewhere with soldiers. Men in uniform. Oh, yeah."

"Knowing you, you'd probably end up in some war zone and get shot," Rosie told her. "Or blown up by a bomb."

"Nah!" Stacey said. "That only happens to soldiers. I wouldn't be a soldier!"

"They could blow you up anyway," Rosie said. That's what happens in wars."

"Like you'd know!" Stacey said. She took out her mascara and started putting it on, her mouth open like a fish's.

"You don't have to be Einstein to know that people get hurt in wars, stupid!" Rosie said. "Just put on the TV and you'll see it happening all over the world."

"OK, then," Stacey said in a huffy voice. "Where don't they have any wars? I'll go there."

Rosie thought the answer to that was quite obvious, but she didn't say anything for a minute while she tried to think of a place Stacey would hate.

"Latvia," she said. "Or maybe the Ukraine."

"Dumps," Stacey said. "Anyway, who cares if war's dangerous? It's so boring round here. A bit of danger would totally spice things up."

"Right," said Rosie, sarcastically. "A few dead people. That's always good for a laugh."

Stacey got up and threw her chip paper in the canal – she wasn't used to Rosie taking the mick out of her and she didn't like it. "I'm out of here," she said, and stalked off.

For a few minutes it felt good to have wound Stacey up a bit, but then Rosie started to get bored by herself by the canal. She walked home through town, taking her time so her mum and her grandmother would have finished their dinner before she got back. When she got in the door they were watching a repeat of a lame old TV programme her grandmother liked. *Last of the Summer Wine*, it was called. It was all about old people.

Rosie went to bed.

Chapter 4
The Front

Rosie must have fallen asleep on her bed, because she woke up in the dark still in her clothes. There was an awful noise nearby, like people moaning. Rosie shot up out of bed, her heart pounding in her chest. What had happened?

"Help! Help!" shouted a voice. It sounded like it was in a lot of pain. Rosie ran to the door.

In the hall it was pitch dark but there was a light on in one of the rooms. She ran to the light, expecting to see her mum or her grandmother lying hurt on the floor. Instead she saw a young boy lying on a bed made of canvas. He had his hands round his leg and he was crying.

"Help me," the boy sobbed. "Please! My leg hurts so bad. I think I'm going to be sick."

Then he was sick. Rosie held a bowl out for him. It was horrible. When he was done she found a wet cloth and wiped his face.

"Where am I?" the boy asked. "Where am I?"

"Poor lad," said a voice behind Rosie. She got such a fright she almost dropped the bowl. When she turned round she saw a long room, lit by lamps here and there, and a row of beds with men lying in them. The man nearest her was holding himself up on his elbow.

"The poor lad's confused," the man said. "They brought him here and put bandages on his leg, but he keeps crying and asking where he is." Once he had finished speaking, the man lay back down with a groan. He had a big bandage on his head.

When Rosie looked further down the room, she saw that all the men looked hurt or sick. Some were making soft moans, as if they were trying hard not to give in to the pain.

Rosie's heart started to race. Had there been an accident? An earthquake or something?

"Cold," the boy in the bed said. Rosie nearly dropped the bowl again. "So cold my bones hurt and my teeth rattled," he went on, like he was talking to himself. "The tea was hot, but it was dirty. Full of grit. It tasted bad. Made me sick."

Rosie had no idea what the boy was talking about, but it seemed the man in the bed behind did.

"It was bad," he said. "They made it out of water from the puddles, I expect. Still, I was always glad of it."

"What was that place I was in?" asked the boy. There was sweat on his skin and Rosie thought that he might have a fever. She put the bowl down and wiped his face again.

"What place?" she asked. "What place do you mean?"

"It was a long ditch," the boy said. "We were standing in it. It was like a drain, full of cold water up to our knees. And there were rats as big as cats. Some of them were alive, but a lot were dead. And there was an awful noise, all the time."

"That was the guns," the man in the bed behind said. "Machine guns. You were in the trenches, lad. At the Front. You're in Flanders."

Flanders? The Front? What was he talking about? Rosie had only a second to wonder before the boy started to shake like mad. Rosie grabbed his hand.

"There was a huge blast," he told her. "It seemed to be all around me. Then there was a sort of shaking and big chunks of earth started to fly up in the air and explode. There were flashing lights and flames, and then it went dark. I thought I had gone blind."

"Shh," said Rosie. "It's alright now." The boy was so upset that there were tears in her own eyes. She rubbed his hand between hers to try to help him stop shaking.

The boy turned his head to look at her. "Jess?" he said. "Is that you?"

"No," said the man. "It's the nurse, lad."

Nurse? Rosie didn't know what he meant. Then she looked at her clothes. She was wearing a long skirt and a white apron almost up to her chin. There was a red cross on the apron. It must be true. She was in Flanders, in World War One!

"I think Jess is the lad's sister," the older man said to Rosie. "He keeps talking about his home in England. It's all any of us think about, to tell you the truth. That last, long, hot summer at home, the year before the war."

"I was in the street," the boy said. His eyes looked like they were seeing something far away. "I was with my friends. We were watching the blacksmith shoe a horse. He was hitting the shoes into shape on the anvil with a hammer. Someone was whistling. That was when the soldiers came through. They looked so fine in their green jackets. We all went to join up straight away."

"How old are you?" asked Rosie. The boy didn't look any older than she was. In fact, he looked younger.

"Eighteen," said the boy.

"That's what he told them," the man said to Rosie. There was a sort of smile on his face but he looked very sad. "They all did it. All the boys. They said they were older than they were. The army knew it was a lie, but they needed soldiers so badly that they took them anyway."

"We had to do our bit," said the boy. "Or else it would have been the end for all of us."

"It was wrong to take boys," the man said to Rosie. "They only did it because the war had turned bad. Last spring they lost more than a million men. And the boys were so keen to fight. They had no idea what it would be like."

"We couldn't stay at home while Britain was beaten," the boy said.

"I suppose you couldn't," the man said to him. "And when one of you went, you all had to go. Nobody would want to be the one left at home while all of his friends were off in Flanders." He shook his head. "You were brave, I have to admit that."

"Me? Brave?" said the boy. He looked more awake now. "No, I'm not brave. After I got here, I couldn't think of anything except how much I wanted a dry bed, a good meal and some quiet. I was never so tired in my life. I was sore all over. And I was starving. I think I would have let them kill me if only they would let me have a good meal and a night's sleep in a dry bed first."

The older man nodded at Rosie. "That's how it was for all of us at the Front," he said. "Hours and hours of drills and chores in a ditch, with your feet deep in the mud. And waiting. Waiting and waiting. It was boring and it was cold. Even when you went to sleep, you had to put something over your eyes in case the rats went for you."

Rosie felt sick when he said that but the boy smiled and turned to look at him. "But there was friendship," he said. "The best on earth. Laughs and jokes. And parcels and letters from home. That's what kept me from going mad."

"A fear shared," the man said to him, "is a fear halved."

"Then we went over the top," the boy said. "Into No Man's Land." He turned to Rosie. "Nothing I could tell you would come close to what it was like, running at the enemy's guns."

"I can't even imagine it," said Rosie. She didn't really want to hear about it, but she knew it would help the boy to tell her.

"It was muddy," the boy went on, "so our feet slipped. The shell blasts looked like stars in the sky but when they fell, they ripped the earth apart. Great spouts of soil and mud went up in the air."

"You must have been so scared," said Rosie. In her mind she heard Stacey's voice, talking about war like it was a good thing.

"It was like a bad dream," the boy said. "Where the shells fell, there were huge holes in the ground. There were corpses in the holes.

Dead men. Dead horses. In the water and the mud. And there was barbed wire. If it got you, it would rip you to bits."

The boy looked like he wanted to stop, but the man in the bed behind nodded. "Keep going, lad," he said. "It's best to say it out loud. Then you can put it behind you."

The boy gulped. "It was dark, but there were flashes of light when the shells went off. Red and yellow light. I saw Mickey fall. Then Eddie Jones. One minute he was there, and the next he was on the ground. He was cut in two. We all ran, right to left to right again, to try to escape the bullets. Then more men fell. Some were my friends. Johnny Milford. Charlie Josephs. Others too."

"Is that when you were hit?" the man asked.

"Yes. It was like a red hot iron in my leg. I fell. It hurt so much I think I screamed. Then ... there were German soldiers, I think. They were standing round me. I think they bandaged my leg. The pain was so bad I kept blacking out. One time I came to I was in a truck. It was bumping around. Then nothing till I woke up here."

When the boy was finished they were all quiet for a moment. He lay back on the pillow and shut his eyes.

"He'll sleep now," said the other man. "Now he's got it out. Good night, Nurse. Thank you."

"No, thank you," said Rosie. "You were very kind to him."

"I have a son his age, at home," the man said. "I hope he never joins up."

Rosie pulled the covers up round the boy, who was asleep now, and went out. As she walked down the hall outside she saw more long rooms with beds, and more nurses in the same clothes as herself. They were all young, perhaps only three or four years older than she was. They looked tired.

One nurse came up to Rosie and spoke to her in French. Rosie was about to say that she didn't speak French but then she found that she could understand her. The nurse was saying that she was going to get some sleep and that Rosie should do the same.

Rosie followed the French girl to another room where the nurses' beds were. As they walked in, they passed a girl sitting on her bed, in tears. The nurse with Rosie patted her back on the way past.

Rosie wondered if someone she loved had been killed.

Chapter 5
Nine Men, or Twelve

When Rosie opened her eyes again it was day and she could see better where she was. It was definitely a hospital, but very old-fashioned, like you would expect in the First World War. All the nurses slept in the same room.

Rosie got up and put on her nurse dress and apron. She wished she had her watch to pin on to her chest beside the red cross. It would be nice to hold it and feel its heat. That way she wouldn't feel so alone.

In the rest of the hospital, there were beds everywhere, each one with a man in it. Many were badly hurt. Some had bandages on their arms and legs. Some had bandages where their arms and legs used to be. Many of those ones lay very still, their faces pale in the harsh morning light, almost as if they were dead already.

Suddenly Rosie felt empty inside. She wanted to help but she didn't know how. Perhaps it was best to start with the men she knew, like the boy from the night before.

The boy was lying back on his pillow with his eyes shut tight, as if he could make himself be somewhere else if he pretended hard enough.

"Good morning," Rosie said. "How are you today?"

The boy didn't say anything, so Rosie tried again.

"My name is Nurse Sands," she said. "What's yours?"

"Jack," the boy said. He waved his hand at the other men, all still in their beds, asleep or staring at the ceiling. "I don't know these men," he said. "Most of them are older than me. I want my mates. Do you know if they're here?"

"I don't know," said Rosie. "Sorry."

"Perhaps they made it back to the lines again," Jack said. "Or do you think they're dead? Is this a German hospital?"

He was getting upset, so Rosie put her hand on his cheek.

"It's alright," she said. "We treat everybody here. Look." She pointed at the red cross on her apron. "Tell you what, I'll try to find out about your friends. What are their names?"

"Terry," Jack said. "Terry Black." Then he jumped like someone had bitten him, and his eyes went wide.

"What is it?" Rosie asked, scared. "Is it your leg?"

"No," Jack said. "I just remembered. I saw Terry. He was lying in the mud. He had a funny look on his face, like he had got a surprise. One of his legs was gone and his guts were all over the place. There was blood everywhere. I tried to talk to him, but he was gone. And the guns ... They just went on and on, like nothing had happened."

Tears welled up in Rosie's eyes.

"Oh, no, don't cry," Jack said, and patted Rosie's hand. Rosie saw that he wanted to cry too and suddenly she realised that it was helping him to comfort her, so she let him hold her hand while she wiped her eyes.

"You want to stop and sob your heart out," he said after a minute, "but they wouldn't want that. The ones who died. They would want you to go on. The Commanding Officer would expect that, too."

"Yes," said Rosie. "I'm sorry I cried." The words came out funny because her mouth was so dry. She shook her head and tried to smile. "I expect you'd all like a cup of tea," she said, and got up to get it. As she filled the cups from a big metal teapot, she looked at Jack's face. He was very good-looking, under all the pain and fear, with blond hair and blue eyes.

He was too young to have seen his friend die like that.

Another nurse poked her head round the door and smiled at Rosie. "We'll change your bandages soon," she said to the men. "I'm sorry we can't give you much for the pain, but you lot aren't the worst we've got here."

"It's alright," one of the other men said. "It's not too bad."

Rosie bit her lip and bent over the tea. How many men had said that, because they knew no one could help, and then died? She got a good look at them all as she handed out the cups. One was so tied up in bandages it took a moment before Rosie realised his left arm was gone.

"No good looking for it, love," the man said with a crooked smile. "I tried that. It ain't there."

"I reckon there are about nine of us here in total," another man added. His bed sheet was propped up like a tent over his legs. Perhaps his legs weren't there either.

Rosie looked around the room. "Twelve," she counted. "I can see twelve men here."

"Yes," the man explained. "We got enough heads for twelve. But only enough eyes for ten, enough arms for eight, or eight and a half. Enough legs for nine, if you don't mind not having the odd foot or two. So, on average, that's nine."

"If we had a really good surgeon you could get about six good soldiers out of us!" another man said. "But they're no good with the needle and thread."

"Good at cutting the bits out, though!" someone added with a smile that was sort of twisted. "Pity nobody's got a proper pattern!"

Rosie didn't know whether to laugh or cry – she didn't know what they wanted, so she ended up doing both.

"You need my grandma!" she said. "She'd fix you up in no time!"

Chapter 6
The C.O.

That night Rosie heard about the Matron. She even caught a peek at her from the other end of the ward. She had a long, grey dress on, just like Rosie's, and a stiff, white hat. She was older, maybe 40 or 50.

"What are you staring at?" the nurse beside Rosie asked.

"That lady," Rosie said. "Who is she, again?"

"The Matron?" said the nurse. "Very funny. Don't let her hear you joking like that. Miss

Edith Cavell likes her nurses to behave well at all times."

She must be another English woman, Rosie thought. "When did she come over here?" she asked.

"Years ago," said the nurse.

"With the army?" Rosie asked.

"No. She was running a hospital where nurses got trained." The nurse looked around before she spoke again, and when she did she whispered. "They say she helps some of the men escape back to England. The ones that can walk. They have a chance of making it to the coast, and then across the Channel."

Rosie realised the nurse was watching her, waiting to see how she would react. She didn't know what to say. Perhaps this was some kind of test? "Do the Germans know?" she asked in the end, then felt stupid the moment after.

The nurse laughed. "God, I hope not!"

Then Rosie knew it was true. And very, very dangerous.

The next time Rosie saw Jack his memory was in a jumble again, but he said his leg hurt a bit less. About the middle of the day Rosie and another nurse helped him stand up, and with the help of a strong stick he was able to limp a few steps. Then he saw that his pyjama jacket was undone and he realised that they had washed and dressed him while he was so ill. He went bright red. Rosie knew that he was so young that the thought of the girls doing that for him was very different to the thought of them doing the same things for other men.

One of the other men started to clap his hands and sing a music hall song about women who took their clothes off in front of men. The others joined in, those who weren't too busy laughing. Rosie smiled to see Jack laughing with them, a bit embarrassed by the rude words, but pleased to belong among the men. They all needed to laugh and joke in order to bear it.

The next day Jack was able to get about a bit on his own, and he went to visit some of the men who were far more badly hurt than he was. Rosie knew he couldn't do much for them, but it was better for him not to be alone. Many of the other men were about Jack and Rosie's own age, others were older, over 20, even over 25.

While Jack went on his visits, Rosie was busy learning about nursing. It was hard. They didn't have the medicines they needed. Some hadn't even been invented yet.

In one ward, there were men who had been gassed. They didn't talk about it much. Rosie learned to recognise it from their rasping coughs and the way they could hardly draw their breath in. Jack told her about the way gas lay low in the air, a greenish colour, and seemed to move slowly with the wind. He had smelled it only once, and been sick after, choking, his chest full of water even though the air was dry.

Jack's leg was healing well. It was only a flesh wound. He had been very weak at first, and dizzy when he stood up, but now the pain was less, in fact some of the time he almost seemed able to ignore it. He started to do small jobs to help Rosie. Nothing skilled, just fetching and carrying.

Late one night one job took Rosie and Jack to the room where very badly wounded officers were. It was much smaller than the other wards and right now there was only one bed in use. Rosie put down the bandages she had brought and looked at the man lying still and quiet in the bed. He was tall and thin with dark hair and his face was very pale. His eyes were blue, very clear, and shadowed around the sockets, as if he had not slept for more nights than he could remember.

"Hello, Jack," he said, his voice little more than a whisper.

Rosie saw Jack turn round, his eyes wide. This man must be his C.O. – his Commanding Officer. Jack looked half happy and half in pain and she could see how important this man was to him, and also that he had seen that he was very badly hurt indeed.

"Hello, sir," Jack said. "Can I ..." He stopped. He looked at Rosie and it was clear that he wanted more than anything else at all to be able to do something for the C.O., but what was there to do? He was helpless.

"Pour him some water," Rosie said.

Jack did it at once, his hand shaking a little. He took it over to the bed, lifted it to the C.O.'s lips and helped him drink. Rosie helped to lift him up so he could take it in. He felt very thin, light, as if his strength were gone.

"Thank you," the C.O. said, and lay back on the pillows. "Made any plans yet, Jack?"

Jack seemed confused.

"To escape," the C.O. said, watching him. "Another few days and you'll be well enough to go. What about the others?"

Jack looked at Rosie. "It's a prisoner of war's duty to escape," he explained.

"What?" Rosie said. "But what if you get caught?" She could feel tears in her eyes. She hadn't looked after Jack all this time only to see him do something stupid.

"Well," Jack said, "if I was caught I would probably be shot. That's what happens to escaped prisoners. I wouldn't be in your warm, safe hospital any more, I would be out in the open, probably being hunted."

"And what if you got away?" Rosie asked. "Where would you go? Home?"

"Oh, he'd get back to the Front Line again," said the C.O. "In time. And then he would go back up over the top."

"No, Jack!" said Rosie. "You did that once already. And look what happened to you! You were shot."

"That's my duty, Ros– er, Nurse," Jack said. "To refuse ... well, that would make me a coward. And that would be worse than being shot. Then I would let down the C.O., and my mates."

Rosie didn't say anything.

"I'm working on it, sir," Jack said. "A way to escape."

The C.O. smiled. "Good. Knew you would be."

Chapter 7
Nurse Cavell

The next morning Rosie was caught by surprise when Edith Cavell herself came around the ward as Rosie changed Jack's bandage.

Rosie looked at her with interest. She was quite old and not pretty in a normal way, perhaps she never had been, but there was a kind of beauty in her face anyway. It was something to do with strength, how sure she was about what she believed, what she cared about. It was as if she had finished worrying about herself and was ready to put all her energy into helping other people.

"You're a lot better, Private Smith," she said to Jack. "Can you walk without too much pain?"

"Yes," said Jack. "No pain at all."

"That's not true," said Rosie. "He does have pain. But he wants to leave, so he lies about it."

Miss Cavell didn't smile with her lips but there was a light in her eyes. "Well, Nurse, thank you for telling the truth."

"I am ready," said Jack. He glared at Rosie.

"I think you are very brave to try to do things so early," Miss Cavell said. "Like the risk you took, joining up at your age ..."

Jack glared at Rosie again and she could see he thought she had told Miss Cavell how old he really was. She shook her head to tell him that she hadn't said anything.

Now Miss Cavell smiled properly, as if she had understood what they were both thinking. "I see a lot of young men here," she said. "So

I'm quite good at telling how old they are.
You're nowhere near 18. It was a brave lie,
and we love you for it. But rushing to escape
before you are strong enough would not only
put your life in danger, it would put everyone
else at risk as well. I'm sure you don't want to
do that." It wasn't a question. In a quiet sort
of way it was an order.

"No, ma'am," Jack agreed. Rosie thought he
looked tired. It must be so hard to do
everything they expected of him, to be what
the C.O. believed of him, what Miss Cavell said
he was. It was so important to him, more than
being safe or warm or having decent food. He
wanted to belong among the heroes, even if
belonging meant dying.

"No, ma'am," Jack said again. "Next week,
then." He was not asking her, he was agreeing,
obeying her order.

Miss Cavell nodded to him. "Goodbye, then.
Nurse, do you have a moment?"

Rosie followed her out. She was a bit
scared that Miss Cavell would tell her off, but
in fact, she smiled. "Well done," she said. "He
isn't ready to go yet. Not for a week or two."

She turned to go, then stopped and peered at Rosie's apron. "Where is your watch, Nurse?"

"I don't have one," said Rosie.

"Here," said Miss Cavell. She took a watch from her pocket and handed it to Rosie. "I have two. Take care of it."

Rosie waited till she was gone, then looked at the watch. It was the same one the man in the shop had given her, back in her own time. As she knew it would be.

Chapter 8

Arrest

The next day, news came that Miss Cavell had been arrested by the Germans for helping prisoners to escape.

The hospital was very quiet all morning. Everyone was too stunned to speak. Rosie felt cold inside, as if she were ill, and she couldn't stop shivering.

About mid-day, a young German soldier came for Rosie while she was in Jack's ward, giving the soldiers tea. The German was only 17 or 18 but he had a gun in his hand. It took all Rosie's strength for her legs not to wobble.

Surely they weren't going to shoot her just because she was British?

But then that was what this whole war was about! Jack shot people because they were German! Rosie had no idea if he had ever killed one, but the Germans didn't know that.

Behind Rosie, Jack stood up. "I'm coming with her," he said.

"No," said the German. He waved his gun. "Just her."

"It's alright, Jack," Rosie said. "I'm not scared, but thank you. You are very brave." She turned and followed the soldier, with tears in her eyes.

They walked up the corridors until the soldier stopped at one door and knocked. There was an answer at once. It was in German but it didn't sound that different from "come in" in English.

Inside there was just one man, in a seat behind a wooden table. He looked very ordinary, with a round face, blue eyes and short, neat hair the colour of straw. His hands were on top of the table, strong and clean.

"Come in, Nurse Sands," he said. It was an order, of course, but he made it sound almost like an invitation. Somehow that scared Rosie even more. She would like to have stood up to him, since he was the enemy, but even as she thought about it, she knew it would be stupid. There was nowhere to run to. She would just look silly, so she sat on the chair facing the German. Closer to, he looked about 40, not a young man at all, and there were tiny lines in his face when he smiled. The markings on his uniform said he was an officer.

"Why I am here?" Rosie asked. She knew, of course. They were going to ask her about Miss Cavell. It felt like there was a cold stone in her tummy and her throat was so tight she choked when she tried to swallow. They might not believe her when she said she knew nothing about any plans, and then they might take her away, too. All of a sudden she understood how Jack felt about being a hero. If only she had helped men escape. Then she would have something to be proud of. Instead, she was just a coward.

"You have worked here for some time?" the German asked.

Rosie forced herself to speak. "Yes, sir." It came out too high. She must get hold of herself and behave with courage – this might be the last chance she ever had. "Yes, sir, I have," she said. That sounded more normal. She looked up and met the German's eyes.

"I hear you are one of the few English nurses left," the German said.

"Yes, sir," Rosie answered.

"Brave girl," the German said. He spoke English very well, with very little accent. "And you are so young. How old are you, in fact?" He smiled, and there was something in it that could have been sadness.

"Twenty," Rosie lied, lifting her chin a little higher. If Jack had lied to his own officers to get into the army, Rosie certainly wasn't going to tell the truth to a German.

The German lifted his hand off the table for a moment as though he wanted to wave away the lie. "It doesn't matter," he said. "I have a daughter about your age." His voice became a little tight as if the effort of control were very great. "I had a son, too. He was a little older. He was killed at Verdun."

"I'm sorry," Rosie said, before she could think. She couldn't imagine how she'd feel if Jack died. Then she remembered she was talking to a German, and she felt like a fool. The Germans were the enemy. It was supposed to be good that one of them was dead!

"Many more will die, I think," the German said. "Unless the fighting stops soon."

"Perhaps it will," Rosie said, and for a moment she knew they both wanted the same thing. Except, of course, the German wanted the war to end because his side had won.

As if he were thinking the same thing, the German smiled. "So you help to care for your wounded. Are you a good British subject, Nurse Sands? Are you loyal to your King and Country?'

"Of course," said Rosie.

The German nodded. "But a Red Cross nurse should not be loyal to any country. So Miss Cavell should not have helped prisoners escape, should she?" It wasn't a question. He knew the answer.

A horrible stillness filled the room. For the first time, Rosie could hear voices outside in the corridor and beyond the window in the open yard.

The German waited.

"She should do what she thinks is right, sir," Rosie said in a low voice, but she did not look away. She saw a flicker of respect in the German's eyes, there for a second and then gone again.

"It must have been a very hard thing to do without help," the German went on. "In fact, I would say it would be impossible."

Rosie didn't know how to answer. She wanted to say something brave and defiant, but the German was so polite and pleasant that that would just look like bad manners. If only he had been rude, then Rosie could have been rude back.

"I expect it would be hard," she said. "Nothing is really easy in war, though."

"No," the German agreed.

This wasn't going the way Rosie had expected. It all seemed so stupid. This German was just like an Englishman. Rosie tried to think of all the things Jack had told her, how all those men had been shot or blown to bits, how Terry had fallen on the ground with his guts hanging out, dead. It was German guns that did that – blew men and horses to bits. But then, British guns did exactly the same. She thought back to her history class and the confusing reasons for the war. It didn't seem any clearer now, here in the middle of it.

"We have to do what we think is right," she said simply.

"I know," the German agreed. "And if we let her go, Miss Cavell would go back to helping British soldiers, wouldn't she? She has helped thousands. British, French, Belgian, even Americans."

Rosie was amazed, struck with wonder and a kind of admiration that filled her with joy. "Really?" she said. "I didn't know that."

The German smiled. "So you didn't help after all. Well, she did a good job if she was working alone. Doesn't make us look very good. One middle-aged woman, without firing a shot, stands up to the German army. You see that we have to stop her."

Rosie tried to think of a way to defend Miss Cavell, but from the German's point of view there was nothing she could say. So she did the only thing she could think of – she tried to reach out to him as a kind man. "I don't think you believe that is the right thing to do," she said.

The German sighed, like he was cross, and yet there was something in his eyes, in the way his shoulders fell, that made Rosie think he was a bit sad, too.

"You may go back to your wounded soldiers, Nurse Sands," he said. "But if you do help any of them escape, remember that it will be our duty to shoot you. Do you understand?"

Rosie stood up, and even though her legs wobbled a bit, she managed to keep her back straight. "Yes, sir."

It was not long after that when Jack came for Rosie and told her that the C.O. wanted to see her.

"Don't stay there long," he said, in a low voice. "I think he's … pretty bad."

Rosie felt a coldness in her stomach. She went because it was Jack who had asked her to, but she was afraid in a very different kind of way.

The C.O. was propped up with pillows, and he smiled when he saw Rosie, but his face was grey and hollow, as if his soul had already half gone from inside his body.

"I hear the Germans sent for you," he said, in little more than a whisper.

"Yes, sir," Rosie said.

"What did they want?" he asked.

"To see if I know anything about Miss Cavell, and how people escaped back to England, sir," she answered. "I told him I didn't."

"Did he threaten you?" The C.O. looked worried and there was pity in his blue eyes.

"No, sir," Rosie said. "He was ... he was sort of fair ... to tell you the truth. He ..." She stopped. She had no idea what to say and she wished she hadn't begun. How could she tell a British C.O. that the German was not a bad man at all? The C.O. was dying, and the Germans had killed him.

The C.O. smiled. "Was he a decent chap, then?" he asked. "He probably has children your age."

Rosie could hardly swallow around the lump in her throat. "He said so, sir."

"But you will help the men to escape, if you can?" the C.O. asked. He blinked as if he were finding it hard to speak, even to keep his eyes open.

"Yes, sir!" Rosie said at once. "Of course I will. I'll find a way."

"That would be the best way to honour Miss Cavell," the C.O. said. Then he tried to say something more, but his voice faded away.

Rosie wanted to cry out, "No! Don't die!" but she knew that a nurse couldn't carry on like that. She had to let the C.O. die like a man, so she stood back and waited.

The C.O. closed his eyes and after a while the smile faded from his lips and he lay still.

Rosie turned and walked out of the room, bumping into the door post and barely noticing it. She went to Jack and shook her head, not even able to tell him. He put his arms round her, and then she cried.

Chapter 9
Waiting

Over the next few days nobody spoke much, except to say "please" and "thank you", "pass this", "turn the light out" – little things that had no meaning except habit.

Rosie knew that crying and being sad would change nothing and would let the others down, so she tried hard to keep her spirits up. In truth she felt very alone. Not only was she in the wrong time, but now Miss Cavell was gone and all the other nurses were afraid.

Rosie spent a lot of time with Jack. He was better and should have been moved on somewhere else, but the hospital was a bit lost without Miss Cavell and somehow he had been forgotten. He was still sad about the C.O. and he told Rosie he felt empty inside, as if he would never be warm again.

Rosie showed him the watch. "Miss Cavell gave me this," she said. "It's hers. I like to hold it and think of her."

Jack took the watch and turned it over. "It says 'E.C.'," he said. "I wonder if there's anything inside." He opened the back of the watch. It was empty.

"I know," Rosie said. "Give me a bit of your hair. Then I'll always remember you."

They cut off a bit of Jack's hair and put it in the watch. "There," said Jack. He shut the back with a snap, and he seemed a little bit different, like that little action had helped him to come to a decision.

"Come on, Rosie," he said. "We need to see the Senior Officer."

"Who is the Senior Officer now?" Rosie asked. "Is it Captain Spooner? Is he alright to talk to?"

"He's not bad," Jack said. "If we can get to see him. I wish I wasn't the lowest rank of solider."

"That's easy," Rosie said. "I'm a nurse. We'll take him some tea."

Captain Spooner was about 23, but to Rosie and Jack that made him an old and wise man. He had been on the Front over a year. They gave him the tea, then stood trying to think exactly how to say what they wanted. Rosie was scared, they had no business doing any of this, but it was as if a tiny part of the C.O. and Miss Cavell's spirit was helping them.

"What is it, you two?" Spooner asked.

"Sir, those of us who can stand have to meet up," said Jack, "and plan a way to escape. I know Miss Cavell has been arrested, but that doesn't mean we should give up the fight. In fact, it's all the more reason why we have to keep going ... sir."

Spooner sighed. "Have you any idea how we can do that, without her help?"

"No, sir," Jack said. "Don't you know?"

Spooner swore under his breath, then drank the rest of the tea. He handed the mug back to Rosie. "I suppose I'd better work something out, then, hadn't I?"

"Yes, sir," said Jack, and he saluted.

That evening Rosie and Jack gathered the able-bodied men together. There were just under a dozen of them strong enough to move around, and possibly escape or at least help others escape. In the dim candlelight their faces showed their fear, and below that the closeness of danger and death.

"How are we going to get past the Germans without Miss Cavell?" someone asked.

"We've got to find a way," was the answer, and everyone nodded.

"We could wait for her to come back," one corporal said. He had lost an arm and still staggered now and then, off balance. "They won't shoot a woman who's not even in the army. It's all just a game, to scare us."

"It's working, then," someone else said. "I'm scared!"

They all laughed.

"We've got to show them," Spooner replied. "If we don't do anything, they've beaten us. And worse, they've made it look as if Miss Cavell is the key to all the escapes."

"She is!" one of the younger men said.

Spooner's voice was sharp. "Well, we'll have to manage without her now. And they probably won't shoot her anyway. The whole world would hate them for that. They say the Americans are doing all they can to get her out."

"The Yanks are helping? What about the Brits?" the corporal said, with a glare at Spooner, then at Jack. "She's one of ours! You mean we aren't doing a bloody thing to help?" His face was twisted with disgust.

"Our side don't want to get involved," Spooner told him. "That would make it worse. I think they'll send her home to England, to make a show of her, so no one else will copy her and try the same thing."

"We've still got to try to get you out," Rosie said in the sudden quiet.

"Yes," Spooner agreed.

No one argued. Now the hospital with its smell of bleach and blood and its memories of pain seemed a warm, safe place. Compared with the outside world, it was. Compared with where they could end up, it was Heaven.

They looked at each other in the yellow glow of the flame. They were all thinking the same thing. It was like waiting to go over the top into No Man's Land, and the enemy fire.

They began to plan, to try to think of any way to escape. One night when she was alone, trying to sleep, Rosie wondered if there was even a way they could rescue Miss Cavell. But of course that was stupid. The Germans wouldn't shoot her. She was a woman. She was a nurse. No one shot doctors and nurses, except by accident. Just like the men that drove the ambulances.

Ambulances, Rosie thought. That's it! Maybe they could hide the soldiers in the ambulances when they left the hospital! Or they could hide in the sheets and blankets that got taken away for washing.

All that night Rosie lay and came up with different ideas for the men to try. She went over and over the ideas in her head so she could keep them straight and tell Jack in the morning. Then she couldn't wait any more, so she got out of bed and ran along to the ward to tell him.

"You're so clever, Rosie!" said Jack. "We forgot you nurses know the hospital better than us!" He hugged her tight. He looked young and happy for almost the first time since they had met and Rosie grinned and hugged him back.

"I'd better get back," she said. Then she let him go.

"Alright," said Jack. He looked a bit sad. Then, without warning, he leaned forward and kissed her.

"I ... I have to go," said Rosie. Her face was red hot.

"Sorry," said Jack. "I shouldn't have done that."

"No," said Rosie, "it's alright. It was ..."
Before she could think of a word, a huge big
yawn stopped her.

Jack looked a bit miffed for a minute, but
then he laughed. "You need to go to bed," he
said. "In the morning we can speak to Captain
Spooner. Night night."

"Night," said Rosie, with a big smile.

Rosie thought she wouldn't be able to get to
sleep with excitement but her eyes closed
almost as soon as her head hit the pillow. She
fell asleep with a smile on her face, thinking of
Jack.

Chapter 10
Home Safe

Rosie woke up to hear a siren of some sort making a loud, shrill sound. She opened her eyes, wincing, and for a moment she had no idea where she was. Then it came to her like the sudden shock of cold water in the face – she was in her own bedroom, and the noise was her alarm clock.

"No!" Rosie said. "No, no, no!" She wanted to be back in the hospital with the soldiers. She wanted Jack.

Rosie's mother popped her head round the door. "Are you alright, love? You were shouting in your sleep. Have you got a fever?" She came in and put a hand on Rosie's head.

"I'm OK," Rosie said, but she felt like crying.

"Stay at home today, maybe?" her mother said.

Rosie did stay at home that day, and the next one too. She didn't exactly feel sick, but she felt sad and low. The dream had felt so real, even more real than her real life. She missed Jack and the others very badly. Now she would never even know if they had got out alive.

In the afternoon, Rosie was sitting on the couch flicking through TV channels when she suddenly realised that Edith Cavell might have been famous. Perhaps she could find out what had happened to her on the net. She went straight over to the computer and opened up Google. She didn't know how to write "Cavell", so at first she tried different spellings until finally she saw a photo of a face she knew. There was a whole website about her!

When Rosie opened the site, her heart thudded in her chest. At the top there were birth and death dates. Edith Cavell had died in 1915. That was the second year of World War One. Although the text was hard to read, Rosie could see the word "shot" in the third line. So the Americans hadn't saved Edith Cavell at all.

Rosie switched off the computer and went over to sit on the sofa. Then the tears came. Poor Miss Cavell! What a horrible way to die.

Later on Rosie had a shower and got dressed, and got a bus into town. She walked to the library and went inside, feeling very nervous. She had never been in a library before.

"Can I help you?" a lady asked. She looked kind.

"I want ... I want to find out about some things that happened in the past," Rosie said. "In World War One. Only ... only I can't really read."

"No problem," said the lady, like people said they couldn't read every day and it was nothing to bother about. "I can help you. Is it for a project at school?"

Rosie nodded and told her that she needed to find out what had happened to Edith Cavell. "I need to know if any other soldiers escaped from her hospital after she was shot," she said.

"OK," said the lady. She took Rosie over to a computer and found the same page Rosie had looked at before. Then she helped her find some other sites, and some books, and look them up. They found out that Miss Cavell had been shot ten weeks after she had been taken away from the hospital. She had been very brave. She had not let them blindfold her, and she had said that she didn't just die for her country, but for God. Her father had been a vicar and she had very strong faith.

They didn't find out anything about Jack and the others, but they didn't find out about any other soldiers from the hospital being shot, either, so Rosie hoped that meant that they had made it out OK.

"Do you have dyslexia?" the library lady asked when Rosie left. "We have a club here you could come to, if you like." She told Rosie the time every week when the club met.

The next day Rosie felt well enough to go to school. The first class was history. Mr Jones bounced in looking pleased with himself. His hair was standing on end as if he had run his fingers through it over and over again. It almost made Rosie like him again, even if he had embarrassed her the last time she saw him.

"Well, everyone, did you all do your homework?" Mr Jones asked. "I want to hear a story about World War One as lived by a character of your choice. So who's first? Steve? Good – on you go."

Steve had made up the story of a young man in the trenches. Rosie thought it was quite good. He talked about fear and cold and pain, and courage and loyalty, and doing the right thing even when you were so scared you were sick. The only thing she didn't like was that his Germans were all baddies like in films.

"Good," said Mr Jones, when Steve finished. "Who's next?"

Laura Webb put up her hand. "I've done a woman's story, sir."

"What?" Gary Hodder laughed. "They just stayed at home and made socks."

"No they didn't," said Rosie. "Sorry, Laura, but can I jump in? Sir, can I talk about Edith Cavell?"

"OK," said Mr Jones. "On you go, then."

"Some women went to war with the men," Rosie said. "They were nurses and ambulance drivers right out there on the front lines. They picked up men so hurt you'd want to be sick just looking at them. But the women worked night and day, and they never gave up, no matter how bad it got. As long as a soldier was still alive, they would go and get him. They got shot at too. They were hungry and cold and tired and scared, but they didn't run away."

Everyone was looking at Rosie and she felt a bit hot, but she plunged on.

"One of the bravest of all was a nurse who helped hundreds of soldiers from many different countries to escape from Belgium. Her hospital was there, right under the noses of the Germans. In the end the Germans arrested her and put her on trial. The Americans begged them to let her go but the Germans didn't listen. They shot her. She wouldn't let them put a blindfold on her and she faced them while they shot her ..." She took a deep breath to try to stop from choking on the tightness in her throat. "Do you know what she said? She said, 'Patriotism is not enough. I know now that I must have no hatred towards any living person'. That's not just courage, it's greatness."

She sat down carefully because her legs were trembling. There was a stunned moment when no one spoke, then Mr Jones nodded his head slowly.

"Well, you were ill, Rosie, so you didn't get the note about the homework. I wanted you to write like you were the person in your story. But that was very good. One would almost think you were there. And well done for choosing Edith Cavell." He looked around the room. "Girls, Nurse Edith Cavell was a role model for women everywhere. She was the very best and bravest person anyone could wish to be. A good example for you too, boys, if you ever forget about the danger and horror of war."

When the class was finished Rosie went out ahead of the others. She wished she hadn't spoken. To them it was a story from the past, but to her it was real, something to be kept in her heart and not shown to people unless they cared just as much. Like the memory of Jack.

Outside she sat down and pulled out the watch from her pocket. As she turned it over in her hand she thought of Jack again. She so hoped he had got home safe after the war.

"Hey," said a voice. "What's that?"

It was Zack Edwards.

"A watch," Rosie said. "It was Edith Cavell's."

"Wow," Zack said. "How come you have it?"

"A man I know loaned it to me," Rosie said.

"For the history project?" he asked.

"Sort of," Rosie said.

Zack sat down beside her and took the watch from her. He was very careful with it. He turned it over and opened the back.

"Look!" he said. "There's hair in it. I wonder if it's hers."

Rosie smiled, but there were tears in her eyes. She had forgotten about Jack's hair but there it was – a single golden lock, curled up in the back of the watch where he had put it.

"Hey, hey, are you crying?" Zack put his arm round her. "You should still be off school. You look really pale."

"I'm fine," said Rosie.

"No," said Zack. "I don't think so. Come on, I'll take you home. I don't have a class till after lunch."

He bent over and pinned the watch to Rosie's coat. Over his head, Rosie could see Stacey and Jade staring at her. They were green with envy.

"Did you know my brother's in the army?" Zack said. "He's over in Afghanistan now. I hope he meets an Edith Cavell if anything ever happens to him."

"He will," said Rosie, then she let Zack take her hand and lead her home.

Barrington Stoke would like to thank all its readers for commenting on the manuscript before publication and in particular:

Robert Barron
Carita Blakeman
Harry Bucknell
Sam Burton
George Clargo
Nathan Cooper
Charlie Cox
Monique Cruz
Vanessa D'Costa
Sue Dearden
Sergiu Dinte
William Edmondson
Lauren Fitzgerald
Charlotte Fletcher
Aidan Gatley
Anthony Gayther

Harvey Gibson
Ben Gillett
Jack Heyes
Tom Houlihan
Diane Hogg
Leon Jardough
Matt Langstreth
Josh Maddock
Sarah Minton
Cassandra Ohonba
Josh Parish
Jon Smallwood
Ian Talbot
Thomas Tonkins
Toni Watkins
Nicole Whyte

Read how it all began ...

Tudor Rose

Out now!